Map Man

Written by Zoë Clarke

Illustrated by Shane Clester

Collins

Map Man maps.

tap
tap
tap

3

Map Man pats.

4

pat

pat

pat

5

Map Man maps.

tap

tap

tap

7

Map Man pats.

pat

pat

pat

Map Man dips in.

Map Man did it.

After reading

Letters and Sounds: Phase 2

Word count: 38

Focus phonemes: /s/ /a/ /t/ /p/ /i/ /n/ /m/ /d/

Curriculum links: Understanding the World: Technology

Early learning goals: Listening and attention: listen to stories, accurately anticipating key events and respond to what is heard with relevant comments, questions or actions; Understanding: answer 'how' and 'why' questions about experiences and in response to stories or events; Reading: children use phonic knowledge to decode regular words and read them aloud accurately

Developing fluency

- Your child may enjoy hearing you read the story.
- You could read the main text on each double page spread and ask your child to read the words in the pictures with actions and using lots of expression.

Phonic practice

- Help your child to practise sounding out and blending CVC words.

  m/a/p   map

  m/a/n   man

  t/a/p   tap

- Look at 'I spy sounds' on pages 14 and 15. Say the sound together. How many words can your child spot with the **p** sound in them? (*picnic, pie, parents, pasta, peppers, pizza, peas, plate*)

Extending vocabulary

- Look at the word **dips** on page 10. Ask your child if they can think of another word instead of **dips** that could be used to describe when Map Man dips into the water (e.g. *flies, dives*).
- Look at the word **sip** on page 13. Ask your child if they can think of another word that could be used instead of **sip** to describe when Map Man sips his tea (e.g. *drink, slurp*).